THE NURSE FINDS LOVE

MAIL ORDER BRIDES OF FIELDER'S UNION

SUSANNAH CALLOWAY

Tica House Publishing

Sweet Romance that Delights and Enchants!

PERSONAL WORD FROM THE AUTHOR

Dearest Readers,

Thank you so much for choosing one of my books. I am proud to be a part of the team of writers at Tica House Publishing who work joyfully to bring you stories of hope, faith, courage, and love. Your kind words and loving readership are deeply appreciated.

I would like to personally invite you to sign up for updates and to become part of our **Exclusive Reader Club**—it's completely Free to join! We'd love to welcome you!

Much love,

Susannah Calloway

VISIT HERE to Join our Reader's Club and to Receive Tica House Updates!

https://wesrom.subscribemenow.com/

CONTENTS

CHAPTER 1

"No."

Sometimes – more often than not, these days – the word *no* seemed to haunt Adele Cowen. Reading over the terse note once more, she gave a shaky sigh and put a hand to her forehead. No matter how many times she looked over the words, there was no changing their message. Once again, her quest for gainful employment in her chosen field as a nurse had been denied – proven to be futile.

That made six. Six demurrals of varying degrees of politeness, in just the past two months. It wasn't that her education was lacking; she'd gone to nursing college at sixteen and had worked in a military hospital for three years after her graduation. And she knew in her heart it wasn't because her qualifications, both ethical and official, weren't up to snuff. After all, in the four years in total she had worked as a nurse, she had developed a reputation for her kindness, her soft touch, her grace under fire.

And she knew, each time she applied for work, it was impossible that the prospective employer could miss how she wore her heart on her sleeve when it came to her vocation. Adele loved people, and there was nothing she wanted more than to take care of them, to help out wherever she could.

It was ironic, now that she thought of it. In the end, it was that desperation to be of use, to fix and save the wounded, that likely kept her from being employed right now. And it was all due to Gerald Foster.

Once more, she heaved a sigh at the thought of his name. How strange to think that his name had once thrilled her to the core, filling her with the hope of a romantic future, of being loved and cared for. Now there was nothing left of her dreams but dust and ashes – and a persistent inability to find work.

She could not put all the blame at Gerald's door. She herself must bear some of it. After all, despite her strong moral upbringing, she had allowed him to persuade her that their engagement was as good as marriage, that they should start their lives together as man and wife before the ring was on her finger, before their vows were properly exchanged. She couldn't help but writhe in embarrassment and shame at the very thought of it. At least, she reminded herself, she'd the moral fortitude to insist they keep to their separate bedrooms; although at times, she felt as though she had been persuaded in so many other ways that the simple act of denying him a shared bed meant nothing in the face of the facts.

It meant nothing to the doctors who turned her down – nothing to the men who heard rumors of her poor reputation and turned her away. Though her virtue was unsoiled, her reputation had no such resiliency, and the doctors in her town in upstate New York would not allow their good names to be linked with that of a woman of known moral weakness.

And though she remained untouched, she could make no argument that would stand against the judgement of the people of the town. Why had she ever let Gerald convince her? Why hadn't she been able to see straight through him to his true motivation?

She crumpled up the paper in her fist, feeling a spark of anger as she looked around the empty flat. It was cramped, bare, scarcely deserving of the term "bedsit." But it had been all that her salary could afford, along with two square meals a day and coal for the winter. And then her former employer had caught wind of her new living situation: allowing a man to whom she was not married to sleep under her roof. The job had ended, her salary had dried up, and Gerald had lasted only a few weeks before he, too, disappeared into nothingness, taking what little savings she had left along with him.

Now here she was, unmarried, unemployed – unloved.

Perhaps that was what made her the most unhappy. She really had loved Gerald, after all, and she had truly believed he loved her in return. That he could be so cold and callous as to abandon her once she was no longer capable of sheltering and feeding him still came as a shock, even two months later.

But there was no point in crying over spilt milk. She stood up from the little table and moved to the window, overlooking the streets of her small town. Unlike the sprawling metropolis of New York City to the south, and Philadelphia to the west, her town of Barton was all too keenly interested in the minute details of everyday life. Surely her choice would have gone unnoticed, had she lived in a larger city – but again, she reminded herself sternly, there was little point in thinking of what might have been.

It was far more important to concentrate on what was happening right now, and what would come next.

Though it was early March, there was still a thin coating of snow on the ground outside. It made her shiver – especially to realize that if she did not find another job, she would be out on the street herself before too long. If she had enough money to pay rent this next week, surely it would be the last time.

But she wouldn't allow herself to be overcome by her disaster. Cold as the world might be, springtime was on the way. Nothing could stop it – and nothing could stop Adele Cowen from moving forward. After all, her mother had always told her she had an indomitable spirit.

Well, the word her mother had more often used was "stubborn." But Adele had known precisely what she meant.

The thought made her smile, the memories of her parents floating to the fore. If only she had the chance to see them again. But it would not happen on this side of life. Her father had died when she was small, and her mother had passed away of a terrible illness only a few years before. Watching someone she loved so dearly fall asleep in death had only strengthened Adele's drive to serve others as a healing presence, nursing them back to health.

On the thought, she reached for the abandoned newspaper that she had plucked from a bench outside her flat that very morning. She had already come across two open positions in the past few months by searching in the paper; perhaps today Fate would smile on her and she would find another.

Several moments of perusing the pages brought her no joy – though it did give her cause for a wry smile as she realized that one of the jobs she had applied for was still unfilled, and the position and was now being offered at higher wages. Well, that was the particular doctor's own fault for turning her down. She would have been glad to work for the lower pay, if only to have something to do.

But there were no other nursing positions that were called for, and she fell to reading the other advertisements, feeling a growing sense of despair.

On the last page, buried amidst advertisements for hair cream and health tonics, was a small box with only a few sentences contained within.

Wanted – a Good Wife.

"What a way to begin," Adele murmured, managing a smile. Rather intrigued, she read on.

Mayor of Branton, Texas, seeks kind, pretty, hard-working, mannerly gentlewoman suitable to be seen on his arm on public occasions without causing embarrassment.

This brought an outright laugh.

"Well. He doesn't want much, does he?"

But it had certainly caught her attention, and she continued to read. After another few words about the mayor, his position, and his needs, the advertisement ended abruptly.

For more information, please write soonest. Care of Franklin Bicknell, Branton, Texas.

Adele put the paper down and eyed it for a moment, one eyebrow raised. Well, it was certainly an interesting proposition. Did she meet all the qualifications? As a nurse, kindness was a large part of her profession, and she felt that it was not an insignificant part of her personality, as well. She certainly knew herself to be hard-working. Her mother had raised her to be mannerly, and she supposed that "gentlewoman" went along with that designation. Also, she had been told, more than once, that she was pretty. She took after her mother, with her light brown hair and hazel green eyes, her rather delicate features and her tall, slim, willowy form. Yes, she supposed she might meet that qualification as well.

As to her ability to avoid causing embarrassment, well – who on God's green earth could guarantee such a thing without knowing the man who was requiring it?

Feeling as though it were all a good joke, she reached for a blank piece of paper and began to write a reply.

Dear Mr. Bicknell –

I happened upon your advertisement in the paper. Upon consideration, I feel that I may very well meet your requirements. Of course, should you request personal references, I understand completely. I have none to offer, as I have few friends in the area and my parents have passed away some time ago. However, I feel confident in saying that I don't believe I would disappoint you – provided that your stated requirements are, indeed, the extent of your requests.

She carried on with the letter, telling him a bit about herself and her willingness to travel to Branton, Texas – wherever that was – in order to marry him. She'd heard of girls who became Mail Order Brides and agreed to arranged marriages, sight unseen, in just this manner. The thought of doing so herself had never crossed her mind.

But here she was, writing the letter – and, she realized, she was smiling to herself all the while. She couldn't help it; it seemed such a ridiculous thing to be doing. But after all, her attempts to gain worthwhile employment had been for naught. She had applied at every doctor's establishment in the entire town. Perhaps it was high time to do something different – perhaps it was high time to do something a little bit ridiculous.

After all, the winter was almost over. Spring was in the air. Changes weren't far off – and they were getting closer every day.

CHAPTER 2

Preston Wilder was certain that the wanted poster was haunting him.

Ever since he had first laid eyes on it, six months before, it was everywhere he looked. Every bank, every post office, every sheriff's office, every mayoral residence. The poster plastered the walls outside each and every saloon, covered holes made by woodpeckers in the doors of general stores, and occasionally blew through the dusty streets like a tumbleweed. Everyone in the Midwestern Territories seemed to be on the lookout for Mike and Vincent Silver, the notorious leaders of the even more notorious Silver Gang. And yet, despite the posters, despite their tendency to pop up every single week in one town or another, no one seemed to be able to find them.

Perhaps it didn't matter so much to everyone else, Preston figured. But to him, it was practically a personal failure. After all, he was a bounty hunter. Finding men who didn't want to be found – men who were figured on wanted posters everywhere – was his job.

Some days, it felt as though it were his only reason for living.

This particular copy of the wanted poster had ended up wrapped around his horse's left front leg as he'd ridden slowly through the last town – a town he couldn't even remember the name of, but somewhere in northern Arkansas. The names of towns meant nothing, other than those he preferred to avoid. And of those, the only one he really cared about was Fielder's Union – Fielder's Union, Arkansas. The one place he had sworn, years ago, he wouldn't be caught dead in.

Idly, looking at the wanted poster in his hand, he thought of how ironic it would be if Fielder's Union was the one place where the Silver Gang had chosen to make their hideout.

"Guess that would explain why I can't find you," he said aloud. As if responding to him, his horse Major shook his head and snuffled.

On the ripped and stained page in his hand, the two outlaws stared back at him. The lower halves of their faces were covered with bandanas, but their features were still rather distinct. Large, hawklike noses, coldly piercing eyes, shaggy dark hair that cut across their foreheads like a series of scars – all of that was clearly discernible even in the inexpert rendering of the artist. On the face of Vincent, the younger of the two, there was a large dark circle running from his temple down to disappear beneath the bandanna. Preston wondered, not for the first time, what the rest of that birthmark looked like.

Someday, he vowed, he would find out.

Meanwhile, here he was with no company apart from Major, hunkered down around a small campfire on the outskirts of – well, whatever the name of the town was. Dogville? It didn't matter. What did matter was that there had apparently been a sighting of the Silver Gang around these parts just a few days before. The thought of finally catching up with them made his heart quicken, the excitement he always felt when he was engaged in the chase. Of course, the reward money was a mite exciting too – he could always use a little extra change, and the Silver Gang had become so odious to the good people of Arkansas that the state itself was offering a considerable reward for their capture, dead or alive. With that money, he could live for years without needing to bring in another bounty.

Or, he thought fleetingly, he could return home, settle down, retire…

He shook the thought off almost as quickly as it had come. Yes, six years of being a bounty hunter was enough to wear any man down. But that didn't matter. He couldn't go home. Not to Fielder's Union.

Then again, his ma was getting older – surely, he should check in on her once every decade or so – suppose she got sick and no one was able to find him, tell him what was going on? Suppose she got so sick that she passed away, and he never even found out until years later?

He gave the fire in front of him a vicious poke with a stick.

Of course, visiting his ma also necessitated that he see his brother – and his brother's wife. And he hadn't seen or spoken to either of them since Annie had broken her engagement to him in order to marry his older brother instead. Oh, she had apologized to him. She'd tried to explain. She'd said that it was love, that the heart wanted what it wanted, that there was no controlling it. But that didn't mean anything. She'd said the same thing to him when they had gotten engaged – this was love. The heart wants what it wants…

Well, her heart evidently hadn't wanted Preston Wilder.

He was so engrossed in his thoughts, in the resurgence of memories, that he didn't even realize the stranger was approaching the fire until he was practically standing at it. Preston's head shot up, eyes narrowed, and he stood up from the log on which he sat, automatically going into a defensive half-crouch, a hand on the pistol at his side. The stranger raised his eyebrows at him and put his palms up and out.

"Now hold on there, mister – I mean no harm. It's just getting a mite chilly out here, thought you'd likely be a friendly sort who wouldn't mind sharing his fire."

Hand still on the butt of his pistol, Preston remained guarded.

"Wasn't expecting to find anyone out here," he said. "Specially not this time of night."

"Ah, well," said the stranger, and gave a shrug. He had a little bit of an accent that Preston could not quite place. The stranger eyed him and made as if to sit down on the ground. Preston nodded, and slowly returned to his own seat on the log. He put his hand to his side, still watchful.

"I hadn't intended to be out here," the stranger said. "Only I was heading in to Dogville for the night, and would you believe it, some bandit stole my horse."

Preston's attention revived.

"A bandit?" he said keenly. "Just one?"

"Oh, there may have been more than one, but it's only one that I saw."

"What did he look like?"

The stranger's eyes slid away from him as he shook his head. Did he look briefly at the wanted poster that sat on the ground near Preston's boots? Preston watched him eagerly, but the stranger showed no sign of recognition.

"It's dark," he said. "Reckon his face was covered anyhow. That's what bandits do, isn't it? Cover their faces so no one can recognize them."

"That's what smart bandits do," Preston agreed. "Of course, then again, they usually get caught anyhow."

"How's that?"

"There are thing you can't hide. Like the shape of a man's nose – the color of his hair – the coldness of his eyes –"

There it was, the flicker of something about to happen. Preston's hand leapt once more to his pistol and he stood up, but the stranger already had a gun pointed at him. Without standing, or seeming to get unduly excited, he gave Preston a pleasant smile.

"Thing is," he said, "I reckoned that a man who would share his fire might also share his horse. What do you think about that?"

"You wouldn't dare," Preston said, heart racing.

"Doesn't take much daring at all, when you've got a gang to back you up," the stranger said affably, getting to his feet. Without taking his eyes from Preston, he bent and picked up the wanted poster. Briefly, he glanced at it, and shook his head with a chuckle.

"Not a very good likeness, is it?"

He held it up beside his face, and Preston held his breath. If he would just look down again, look away, just for long enough that he could get out his pistol –

But the outlaw – Mike Silver himself – didn't play along with his plans. He crumpled the wanted poster up into a ball and tossed it onto the fire.

"Reckon you're that bounty hunter they say's been on our tail for the past six months," he said. "Reckon you're thinking about your earnings, thinking you've caught me now."

"I don't count my chickens before they hatch," Preston said.

"Smart man," said Mike Silver with a grin, and as Preston threw caution to the winds and lunged, Silver pulled the trigger. Preston felt an enormous weight and pressure, something huge and impossibly strong, push him back and to the side and he fell to the ground. Something was sitting on his back, pressing him down, not letting him get up. He knew he had been shot, knew the warm wetness he could feel was his own blood leaving his body. Mike Silver stepped over him and spoke to someone he could not see. He couldn't see much of anything, now.

"Mount up," he said. "Reckon Johnny can have his own horse now, Chente. Not this one, though – give mine to him, and I'll take the chestnut. He's a looker, that horse – he could win prizes." He nudged Preston with the toe of his boot. "Not much like his owner, here. Thanks for the horse, smart man."

There was noise after that – laughter and hoots and chatter and the sound of horse's hooves pounding into the distance. But Preston heard none of it.

He heard nothing at all.

CHAPTER 3

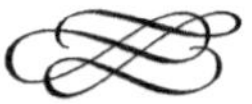

My dear Miss Cowen,

I'm thoroughly pleased that you have chosen to accept my offer of marriage. Though we have only exchanged a few letters, I was able to discern at once that you were ideally suited to my requirements for a wife. Of course, I imagine that some education will be necessary once you arrive, in order to ensure that you are properly trained for life as a mayor's wife. But nothing too onerous will be demanded of you.

Branton is a quiet, idyllic little town. Unlike much of the West, we never suffer the raids of bandits or the attacks of outlaws. I'm absolutely certain that you will find it a peaceful life here in Texas, and provided that we get along well, our future is bound to be pleasant in the extreme.

Of course, I would prefer that you do not continue with your official work as a nurse once you are my wife. However, I am not an unreasonable man; though there is no need for you to bring in an income, should you choose to proclaim nursing as your vocation and continue to nurse ailing members of my community, I would not stop you. Provided that you do it strictly on a volunteer basis, of course. We can't have it be said that the mayor of Branton cannot provide for his wife's needs. But a volunteer spirit is always appreciated, and I daresay it will do much toward enhancing your reputation in the town.

I've sent the money for the train ticket west. It will take just over a week for you to arrive, and I assume you will leave as soon as possible after you receive this. I'll look out for you at the station in Branton on the afternoon of the twentieth of April.

Until then,

Yours respectfully,

Mayor Franklin Bicknell

Adele folded the letter and returned it to her handbag. Despite herself, she couldn't help but let out a small sigh. Yes, she had made her decision – it had only taken a single response to her initial letter of inquiry for her to make up her mind. Mr. Franklin Bicknell – Mayor Franklin Bicknell, as he seemed to like to remind her – was undoubtedly a bit on the pompous side. But his letters seemed to contain a bit of sly humor, as well, just as she hoped the advertisement had done. If he had a sense of humor, then she was convinced she could deal with any other unforeseen circumstances her marriage might present.

Besides, what were her other choices? It wasn't as though she could simply stay in New York interminably without an income.

No, agreeing to become the wife of the mayor of a small town in east Texas seemed much the better of her limited options. And he didn't even mind if she continued nursing, provided she did not accept a paid position to do so. Well, that idea did not bother her in the least. She loved nursing, regardless of whether she was being actively compensated for it on a monetary basis; the gratitude and continued health of those she had cared for over the years were more than compensation enough. And, as he had taken care to mention, providing her steady, practiced hand in the community would enhance her reputation – and his, too, she had no doubt.

Yes, heading west was surely the best course open to her. Even if she did have to convince herself of that fact several times throughout the day.

And the journey was coming to an end more rapidly than she would have thought. She was unsure of where she was, precisely – the train was speeding through flatlands at the moment, but there were mountains in the distance. She frowned thoughtfully at them; her grasp on geography was not the best, and several days on the train had all but eradicated her proper sense of time. She supposed there must still be a day or two to go before she arrived in Texas.

There came a short whistle blast from the lead car of the train, and a moment later she could feel the speed of the chugging beneath her begin to reduce. They must be approaching another town.

"Fielder's Union." announced the conductor, entering her car and passing through. "All for Fielder's Union, make ready. Fielder's Union, Arkansas."

Adele turned her attention back to the window. It didn't sound like a very interesting town.

Something rather interesting was happening outside the windows, however. There were several men on horseback approaching the train at a great rate, leaning forward over the necks of their mounts, half-standing as if to urge the horses on. The lead man rode a pretty dark brown horse with a magnificent black mane, tossing in the wind. Adele watched, intrigued and curious. The riders thundered past her as the train slowed even more, and suddenly there was the muffled sound of a bang. The train lurched, the brakes screeched and squealed, and they slid to an unexpected stop.

The conductor dashed back in. His face had gone pale.

"Everyone, remain calm." he said, though he himself was far from this suggested state. "If we remain calm, we'll all be just fine. Just fine." He sounded as though he were trying to convince himself more than anyone else. Adele leaned forward, reaching out to him.

"Excuse me, sir – what is it? What's going on?"

He turned unfocused eyes on her.

"The Silver Gang," he said. "It's the Silver Gang."

Though she had not heard of the gang in question, Adele felt her blood grow cold. She knew what it meant. The train was being robbed. The muffled bang had been a gun shot. Their lives were in danger.

She was just about to stand up, unable to sit still any longer, when the door to the car was flung back and a man entered. He was tall and rangy, and wore a bandana tied over the lower half of his face. His hat was pulled low, and she could see very little other than a thatch of reddish hair that poked out from beneath at the back of his head. His clothes had once been black but were now brown from dust and dirt, and he moved as though he owned the train car. The gun in his hand testified to the validity of his manner.

Cold eyes swept over her, lingering a little – but it was obvious that she had nothing valuable to offer him, and he moved on to the couple who sat in the seats across from Adele.

They were a young couple, well-dressed, the husband with a well-trimmed beard and a waistcoat, the wife with a delicate pink dress and a folded parasol set to one side. Adele could not fault the bandit for turning away from her and focusing on them; everything about them suggested a well-to-do family with spoils for the taking.

The gun was turned on them.

"A likely-looking set of folks," the bandit rumbled. "What've you got for me, mister?"

The young, bearded man stood up, fairly vibrating with fury. "Not a thing, you varmint."

"Is that so?" With a movement that was snakelike in its quickness, he reached past the young man and snatched his wife by the arm, pulling her up to her feet and dragging her toward him. The young man gave a shout and reached out to protect her. Adele saw the man fall before she registered the sound of the blast; the gunshot spun him around and dropped him first to the seat upon which he had been perched. Legs suddenly boneless, he slumped to the ground. His wife shrieked.

The bandit laughed and took the woman's handbag from off her wrist. After a second of thought, he took her hand in his and yanked her wedding ring from her finger, too.

"Anyone else want to give me a try?" he asked the scattered denizens of the car, all of whom were watching him, hushed and frightened. No one said a thing. He laughed again, shook his head, and turned back toward the door he'd entered from. "Cowards, that's what you are. Nothing but well-heeled cowards."

The young wife collapsed to the floor next to her husband, sobbing. Without thinking, Adele lurched across the aisle toward them, getting to her knees alongside the fallen man. She felt for his pulse, turned his head toward her to make sure he did not choke on his tongue, and put pressure on the wound with both hands.

"He's not dead," she told the wife. "He may pull through if we're able to get help."

The wife, clearly in shock, simply shook her head, eyes wide.

Adele reached out a hand and put it on her arm.

"Trust me," she said. "I'm a nurse. I can help. Now, I need more cloth to help cover the wound. What do you have with you? Will you look, please, and I'll tell you what will work best."

Doing her best to remain calm, she talked the young woman through what she wanted her to do. The wife obeyed, her hands shaking as she undid the clasps of her case. She moved slowly. Wildly, Adele looked over at the few other passengers on the car, but they were all staring still at the door where the bandit had entered. Adele turned to look, and her heart leapt into her mouth. There stood the bandit, just on the other side of the door, and his cold eyes were fixed on her. He watched for a moment, and then turned and went away.

Her heart hammering and her breath coming shallowly, Adele returned her attention to the man on the floor beside her. She could do nothing about the bandit, what he might do, what he might plan – she could only do her best to help the ailing and the injured.

In the distance, she heard more muffled gunshots. Someone must be fighting back – at least, she hoped that was the case.

Despite the amount of blood that the young, bearded man had lost, the situation was not as dire as it had first appeared.

"Very good," Adele told his wife, striving her best to remain calm. "You see, there's some color coming back to his face. We're near the town – as soon as this is over, we'll be able to get him to a doctor. You'll see. Everything will be just…"

The door to the car opened and another bandit stepped in. This one she recognized, vaguely; it took her a moment to realize that he must have been the one who was leading the charge, riding the beautiful dark brown horse.

His eyes, equally as cold as those belonging to his fellow gang member, swept over the situation in front of him and lighted on Adele. He snapped his fingers at her.

"You," he said. His voice was rough, but it was rough from urgency, rather than cruelty. He beckoned to her with his hand. "Come here."

"What? Me?" Adele faltered.

"I hear you're a nurse."

"—yes…"

"Well, I've got a man in need of nursing. Get up."

Adele looked to the young woman who still sat crouched beside her. They exchanged a wide-eyed glance. As frightening and difficult as it was to be responsible for the young man who was still bleeding and in serious danger, crouching here beside the unknown woman seemed much the safer, friendlier option.

The bandit did not wish to wait for her to make up her mind, however. With an impatient grunt, he pulled his pistol from its holster and pointed it at her.

"Now," he demanded.

"No, please," whispered the wife.

Adele took in a deep breath.

"Come here," she said, trying to stay calm. "Put your hands here, where mine are. Just – keep pressing down. He may wake up soon, and he'll be in pain. Talk to him. Tell him that everything will be all right. Soon, you'll be able to get to a doctor, and he will see to you." She put a bloody hand on the young woman's shoulder, and stood up, managing to give her a brave, if somewhat watery, smile.

"Thank you," whispered the young wife.

Adele turned to face the man, her fists balled at her side.

"Where is the man who needs care?"

In two steps, he was at her side. He gripped her arm and pulled her along with him.

"Outside," he said. "Waiting."

Adele gave a yelp as the outlaw turned to the exit of the car, yanking her behind him. There was no escaping the firmness of that grip. Before she knew it, he had pulled her out of the car, down the steps, and was lifting her up onto the beautiful horse she had seen before. Then he was up behind her, and with a kick to the horse's ribs and a wordless call, they were away. Behind them, the other bandits came along, in various stages of disarray.

As she rode away from the train, the outlaw's arms firmly clamped around her, Adele could not help but wish that she had tried just a little bit harder to find employment back in New York.

CHAPTER 4

Preston Wilder sat back against the rock formation near the dry riverbed, looking off toward the lights of Fielder's Union as they turned the cloudy skies above a vague purple. He shook his head and sighed.

"Here we are, April in Arkansas," he said. "And what've we got? Tornado weather, of course." He stared upward at the stormy skies. He didn't really think that there would be a twister; the skies lacked that sallow, evil quality that came before the worst storms. At least, that was how it had been when he was a youngster, growing up here in Fielder's Union. Now, after six years away, he was inclined to doubt his memory. If a twister came, maybe it would just sweep away the town – and with it any stubborn inclination on his part to go home, see his ma, maybe even make amends with his brother and Annie…

No, he didn't want to. And if he didn't want to, he didn't have to. He had come here looking for the Silver Gang, that was all there was to it. He certainly wouldn't have returned to the vicinity of Fielder's Union for any other reason.

His ribs ached. Slowly, still feeling the soreness of his battered body, he lifted a hand and placed it over the bandaged patch. If the bullet had been a little higher, he would have been dead. If he hadn't awoken before he bled out, he would have been dead. If he hadn't managed to drag himself back to Dogville, he would have been dead. If some kind passerby hadn't located the elderly doctor in time, he would have been dead.

If the doctor had insisted on payment upfront, as some doctors were known to do – Preston wouldn't have blamed him, for he knew that he looked mighty shabby and probably pretty broke, too – then Preston very well would not be alive to sit there outside of his old hometown, nearly a month after being shot, knowing that he was yet again hot on the trail of the man who had shot him. The Silver Gang. Just a week earlier, they had struck again – and now here he was, sitting and waiting, as though they might decide to pay him a call at his campfire for a second time.

It had worked out pretty well for them the first time, after all, he thought ruefully.

His ribs ached, his back ached, his arm ached, and he felt a bit lightheaded. He frowned, reaching for a stick to stir up the fire and finding that his fingers closed on nothing. He sat up, taking in a few deep breaths. Maybe he hadn't recovered as fully as he would have liked. The doctor had been very elderly, after all, and Preston wasn't entirely sure he'd known what he was doing.

Elderly – like his ma was getting elderly. A twinge of guilt stabbed at him, and he glanced swiftly to the west of the town in front of him before he could stop himself. To the west was the little ranch where he had grown up. The little ranch he would have owned half a stake in, if he'd decided to stick around in Fielder's Union. The little ranch with the small cottage behind the ranch house, where he had dreamed of settling down and raising a family with Annie, once upon a time…

Now that house belonged to James, and Annie was the mistress of the household. Despite the ache that it caused, Preston fell to speculating about their lives together. Would they have children by now, a passel of little ones running around smudging dirt on the furniture and rumpling the rugs? Would the kids look more like James – tall and spare and rather gaunt of face – or like Annie – small, with a round dimpled face and the sweetest smile he'd ever seen…

His thoughts seemed to be running away with him. For a moment, he could have sworn he could see them, see the children that he wasn't even sure existed, dancing around the fire. He sat up straight, his heart pounding, ready to call out to them to watch out or they'd get burned – but there was no one there, of course.

He shook his head, irritated with himself, and got on his hands and knees to come closer to the fire. He was so cold – it shouldn't be this cold in April, especially not during tornado weather. The breeze that picked up brought a cooling touch to his clammy forehead, and he clenched his teeth, trying not to shiver.

He pulled his wool blanket around his shoulders.

He ought to go and see his ma. Forget James and Annie – they could please themselves. Well, they had, hadn't they? But it didn't matter. They'd been married for six years now. They were practically an old married couple. The romance must be gone by now, he was sure of it. If he saw them, he reckoned he would just laugh.

He wasn't bitter, though.

Still, none of it was his ma's fault…

He should go and see her.

If he caught the Silver Gang, he promised himself. If he caught them, he would do just that. He'd go and see his old ma. He'd even be kind and generous to James and Annie, too. Maybe he'd use the bounty money to buy new hats for all of their children.

But that was later. Now, he had to get control of this shivering. Maybe if he lied down for a little while and pulled the blanket over him. Maybe he could just close his eyes, and the strange floating lightheaded feeling would go away. Maybe when he awoke, Mike Silver would be sitting across the fire from him, begging him to arrest him, to bring him to justice, to take him away from this life of crime.

CHAPTER 5

It seemed like forever that they rode along in the darkening countryside, as the sun dropped below the horizon and the stars spangled the velveteen skies above. Though it was hard to make out any details what with the jouncing of the horse, Adele had the impression that there were lights somewhere ahead of them. Perhaps the town at which they were scheduled to arrive – Fielder's Union, wasn't that what it was called? She wondered whether the train had made it yet, and whether the young couple had found the doctor. She could only hope; if they had not, she was terribly afraid that the bearded young man had left his wife a widow by now.

But she had to cling to hope – hope that the poor man would be all right, and hope that she would be, too.

They seemed to be skirting the edge of the town; which made sense, of course. The last thing the outlaws would want to do was ride straight into the middle of civilization, after just having robbed a train. At long last, the man behind her pulled back on the reins and drew the horse to a halt. Around and behind them, she heard the sounds of a dozen other horses doing the exact same thing. Then the bandit swung himself down from the saddle. She had scarcely a second to realize what was bound to occur when she felt his hands clamp on either side of her waist; he lifted her down from the saddle as though she weighed no more than a feather and deposited her with a teeth-rattling jar on the ground.

"Kim, start a fire. Mark, Sam, you're in charge of accounting. Chente, come over here." He took Adele by the arm and led her toward the sparking flame that was the beginnings of a campfire. The bandit named Kim was evidently proficient at his task; it was but a matter of seconds before there was enough light to see by. The leader of the gang pushed her to sit beside the fire, and another man came and sat beside her. He moved slowly, sluggishly, and sat with his head low. This, evidently, was her patient.

"He's got a cut on the side of his face," said the leader, squatting on the other side of the injured man and eyeing him critically. "Chente, turn so she can see. I wouldn't do that, if I were you," he added swiftly as Adele moved her hands to the bandanna around the man's face. She looked at him, and he caught her gaze with his, eyes cold and direct. He nodded. "Leastways, if you want to see another dawn – I'd suggest you prevent yourself from seeing too much."

She swallowed hard.

"It'll be rather difficult to treat a wound if I can't see it."

The outlaw leader nodded, but his acknowledgement seemed to make no practical difference.

"Do it," he said.

Adele bit her lip and returned her attention to the man in front of her, the one called Chente. Taking him by the chin, she turned his head so she could see the wound. The entire half of the man's face was covered in blood; blood had soaked the bandanna and dried, and she knew that peeling it off was going to be painful anyhow. Doing her best to keep her voice calm and steady, she requested the supplies that she needed to care for the wound.

Clean rags and a bucket of water were brought to her. She heated the water until it was near boiling, and then set to work. After several moments of cleaning and complete silence from the wounded man, she let out a breath.

"It's not as bad as it looks," she said. "It's deep, but it will heal provided he has stitches." She looked back at the leader. "I'll need a needle and thread."

The leader tossed a glance to another one of his men, who wordlessly obeyed. It took a while for him to come back with the required objects. The fact they had them at all was surprising to Adele. Were they shot at or wounded regularly to carry such supplies?

She held the needle to the flame for a moment to clean it, and then resumed her duties. Under the pricking of the needle, the man finally began to flinch at last.

She tied it off neatly and smoothed the pad of her finger over the stitches, carefully. For a moment, her touch hovered over the large, circular birthmark that discolored the man's temple and cheek; it disappeared into the bandanna, too, and she could not be sure of the true shape of it. Chente jerked his head away from her and the outlaw leader stood up as though a decision had been made.

"Right," he said. "You did your job well, nursey – I'll let you live. Come on, Vincent." He gave a hand to the injured man, helping him to stand. His manner was markedly different with this particular outlaw among the others of his gang, and Adele could not help but wonder at their connection. There was something similar about them – perhaps they were brothers? The two loomed over her, and she gulped hard, getting shakily to her feet.

The wounded man eyed her, speaking to the other without looking away.

"She's good, Mike – pretty, too."

"Don't tell me she's turned your head."

"Not me," the younger man denied. "But the boss was looking for a lady, wasn't he?"

"That he was…" The outlaw leader reached out and cupped her cheek with his hand, staring hard at her for the briefest of seconds; then he shook his head with a regretful sigh. "No, pretty as you are and pleasant though it would be to have you along with us, you'll only slow us down. The boss'll have to look elsewhere." He turned swiftly to another man. "Jake, the fire."

The bucket of water was refilled and sloshed over the fire, which sputtered and began to die. In the gloom of new night, Jake went for more water to get the fire out completely. Adele clutched her arms about herself. She couldn't help but wonder what the exchange had meant – did they have another employer? Was the gang being organized by someone else entirely?

And were they really about to leave her here?

"What about me?" she said.

"You'll live," said the outlaw leader in the dark, and he gave a guffaw. "Only because I'll allow it – but you'll live."

"But we're in the middle of nowhere."

"There's a town not far off. You can get there on foot."

She held herself tightly. It was not cold, not really, but with the sudden dark, realizing that she would very soon be utterly alone, the coldness was in her mind.

"Thanks for the help, nursey," said the voice of the leader of the gang. "Be seein' ya."

Jake threw a second bucket of water on the fire, which gave up the little remaining gumption it had left and died out completely. In the dark, Adele stood and shivered, hearing the sounds of the outlaw gang mounting the saddles, whispering to their horses, and finally riding away. She stood there alone and let her eyes adjust to the dimness, slowly, slowly, listening to the hoofbeats dying into the distance.

Then there was nothing but the stars overhead, and in the distance, a faint flickering, as though someone had lit a fire hours before and had forgotten about it.

CHAPTER 6

When Preston Wilder next awoke, he knew for a certainty that he was very ill indeed. It wasn't just that, instead of shivering, he was now burning alive, sweat pouring from him and heat radiating from every inch of his skin. It wasn't just that he still had that terrible, sick-making sensation of dizziness and floating, as though the world was spinning beneath him even though he was absolutely still on the ground. No, the single factor that told him that things were worse than he had feared was that he was hallucinating, and hallucinating in a most unusual way.

There was no way on earth, for instance, that the beautiful girl crouched over him was real.

No, he had to have invented her.

Her brown hair was pulled back in some complicated and undoubtedly fashionable knot, but locks of it had escaped here and there and framed her pale, oval face. Her eyes, fixed on his, were wide and hazel green, unusual both in their color and in their clarity. Her features were delicate and pretty, and her touch on his arm, skating down to his ribs, was practiced and tender.

"Can you hear me?" she said. "Please, don't fall asleep again."

He tried to concentrate. Yes, she must be a hallucination, but that was no excuse for rudeness. Besides, she was by far the most attractive hallucination he had ever had. If he could avoid falling asleep, as she had asked, then he could enjoy every moment of it.

"'m sorry," he mumbled. "I didn't mean to."

"No, no, don't apologize – it isn't your fault." She pressed a hand to his forehead. For a hallucination, she had a very firm grip. "You're very sick. You have a fever – are you injured?"

Her hand ran over his ribs again, clearly feeling the outline of the bandage beneath his shirt. He couldn't help but wince, and she lightened her touch, becoming gentler.

"I'm a nurse," she said, speaking slowly and clearly. "May I examine the wound?"

He closed his eyes and averted his head; she took this as acquiescence, evidently, for the next moment he felt the edge of his shirt, already untucked from his trousers and lifted up.

She ran light fingertips over the bandage, and he let out a slight moan of pain.

"Oh, dear," she said, and he opened his eyes in time to see her shaking her head. "Yes, I'm afraid the wound is badly infected. You must have been sick for some time – it hasn't been dressed properly. I can see that at once."

She put a hand to her forehead. Even in his confused state, it struck Preston as decidedly strange to realize that the beautiful nurse hallucination had hands stained with dried blood. Part of it flaked off as she lowered her arm once more.

"And I don't have anything to dress it – or to clean it…" She looked about herself and shook her head again. "Do you have a flask, mister… oh, goodness, I don't even know your name. I'm Adele. Adele Cowen." She touched his hand, a gentler variant of a handshake. "Can you tell me yours?"

"Wilder," he managed, just able to get the words out clearly. "Preston Wilder…"

"I'm pleased to meet you, Mr. Wilder. Perhaps not under these circumstances – but all the same, I'm glad not to be alone." There was truth in her eyes – as much truth as any hallucination could rightly have, he reckoned. She did look glad to have him for company, as shabby company as he might be. "Do you have a flask? I suppose – oh, never mind, I see it there…"

She was moving, reaching for his flask of whiskey, and then there was a flash of heat and pain, and he closed his eyes again. When he opened them, the stars had moved overhead, he was sure of it. He wondered how many years it had been. Adele Cowen sat beside him, head bowed, eyes closed. She had fallen asleep sitting up.

"Very persistent hallucination," he muttered, and closed his eyes again.

The next time his eyes opened, they were greeted with the early morning light of the approaching sun. The fire had long since died and was giving only a few curling wisps of smoke. The bandage was gone and his half-healed skin over the bullet hole was on fire, but he felt much less as though his head was going to detach and float away.

Adele Cowen, alerted by his stirring, woke up and moved to sit closer to him. He couldn't help but note there were telltale marks on each cheek – the dried streaks of tears. Without understanding, without knowing her circumstances, his heart went out to her all the same.

"You're awake," she cried. "Oh, goodness, you don't know how happy I am to see you. Mr. Wilder, I'm afraid you're still very ill. We've got to get you somewhere that I can patch you up – I did my best, but you're in desperate need of care." She glanced to the east. "I know there's a town nearby here – I believe it's called Fielder's Union."

He flinched; he couldn't help it. She picked up on it right away.

"Perhaps you know of it…"

"I do," he managed to mutter. "Grew up there – my… my mother lives near it."

"Wonderful." She sat up straight and put a hand on his arm. "We should go there right away, Mr. Wilder. I'm afraid I can't promise you'll recover if we delay any longer – you've got to get care."

Presto held his breath for a moment. He could feel the stubbornness resurging, the feelings he had wrestled with last night – and for the six years before that, too. Going home was going to involve pain, anger, guilt, shame, embarrassment – a whole host of emotions that he didn't want, and that he had spent the last six years trying to outrun.

Seeing his hesitation, Adele Cowen softened her touch. Her voice turned pleading.

"Please, Mr. Wilder. Please – I've nowhere else to go."

He met the gaze of those wide, clear, beautiful eyes – and his heart melted, along with a portion of his pride.

"All right," he said. "I've got to get up."

She helped him, and he allowed himself to lean on her more than he might have if they had met under different circumstances. She was stronger than she looked; her tall, seemingly frail form supported him to stand without a moment of hesitation. Together, arms around each other in an embrace that would have been shocking for two so recently introduced individuals – had one of them not been on death's door – they faced in the direction of Fielder's Union.

Preston took in a deep breath.

"Well," he said, still somewhat dazed, "let's go home."

CHAPTER 7

The journey was far longer and more painful than Adele would have thought – not just for the stranger she had met only the night before, but for herself as well. She wasn't injured, of course; but she was completely exhausted. She hadn't eaten since the morning before. Her train had been robbed, she'd been abducted, she was covered in other people's blood, and she had spent a largely sleepless night out in the wilderness of Arkansas in the company of a strange and very ill man who evidently clung to the persistent belief that she was a delusion caused by his fever dreams. Now here she was, her arms around him as though they were lovers, and for every slow and painful step of the way, she took the burden of his weight on her shoulders and helped him to take another.

Her spirit, shaken by exhaustion but unbreakable in the face of the needs of others, was positively encouraged. Yes, things were certainly not as she had expected – but over the course of the last day, she had nursed not one, not two, but three men who were in dire straits. The fact that they were complete strangers who were unlikely to ever repay her for her actions was something of an icing on the cake.

This one, in particular, was rather intriguing. Of the three she had cared for in the past day, he was the first that she'd been able to put a name to. Preston Wilder – it was a rough sort of name, and when he spoke, it was with a rough sort of voice. Despite his illness, he was evidently someone who was used to speaking straightforwardly, getting things done, a man of action. She couldn't help but wonder how he had come to be sitting by a fire in the middle of the night, delirious from fever; especially now that she knew he had family not far away.

But his circumstances were not the only intriguing thing about him. As soon as the day had begun to dawn and there had been enough light to see by, she had reexamined his wound, doing her best to keep it clean and dry. Then she had glanced up, and her gaze had fallen on his features – and remained there for some moments until suddenly his eyes had opened and she had looked away hastily, blushing a bright, hot red.

She couldn't remember ever having seen such a handsome man.

Adele was not used to such thoughts. Though she did not consider herself immune to the attractions of men, she'd never given those around her much thought. Her few friends back in the state of New York had married rather stodgy, prosaic, practical men; she respected them, but that sort of man certainly wasn't her romantic ideal. She supposed she had given up on her romantic ideal entirely, simply by agreeing to marry Franklin Bicknell; she doubted that he would turn out to be more romantic in person than he was via his letters, though she supposed there was always room for hope.

But somehow, having hardly exchanged a word with this man she now helped to limp across the wilderness, she was struck by his presence on a level so deep she hadn't suspected its existence. Perhaps it wasn't so surprising, after all – he was handsome, wounded, she'd cared for him through the night after recently escaping a thrilling – terrifying – adventure...if those weren't romantic circumstances, she didn't know what might qualify.

She continually pushed the thoughts away as they made their way through the early morning countryside. After all, she was set to marry Mayor Bicknell. She had no right to look at any other man; she had no right to even notice how handsome he was, let alone dwell on it.

Still...the thoughts were persistent.

Trying to distract herself from the warmth of his back under her arm, she said, "How much further do you suppose it is?"

He shook his head.

"Not far…" It was clear that anything more than 'not far' would be 'too far,' but he struggled on anyhow. She was intensely grateful when he lifted an arm and pointed to the left. There, just on the other side of the field, was a long, low ranch house, with a barn beside it.

"Oh, thank goodness."

But Preston Wilder said nothing.

They hobbled along together, and it was obvious that he was growing more and more exhausted with each step. Finally, as they drew close to the yard, Adele called out.

"Mrs. Wilder. Hello? Anyone."

A few moments passed as they drew closer, and then the screen door on the porch opened. A head of silver-gray curly hair poked out.

"Yes?" called the older woman, in tones of confusion – but suddenly the door was flung back, and she came out of the house completely, fairly tripping down the steps to reach them. "Preston. Oh, Preston, is that really you?"

"Hi, Ma," Preston Wilder managed weakly, and to Adele's amazement he even mustered up a smile. His smile, wan and tired though it was, was strikingly appealing, and she felt her heart thump a little more heavily. In the next moment, the older woman had reached them. She took up a position on the other side of Preston and mimicked Adele's stance, putting an arm around the man and helping him forward.

"What on earth has happened? How did you come to be here?" In her voice, excitement at seeing her son warred with mystification as to how he had suddenly appeared.

"I'll explain it all, Ma – let's just get inside, I need to sit down…"

"Fall down, more like," said his mother worriedly. She leaned forward to peer around him at Adele. "I'm so sorry, I don't know who you are."

Adele smiled at her.

"That's quite all right – neither does your son. My name is Adele Cowen, I'm a nurse – and it's quite a story."

"Well, Nurse Cowen, perhaps he's right, and we should get him inside first."

As they started the laborious process of getting him up the steps, another woman appeared at the door, stepping out to hold it open. She was young, perhaps a handful of years older than Adele herself, and had a comfortable plumpness to her that spoke of happy living. Her eyes were as worried as those of Preston's mother, and when the young man looked up, their eyes locked for a brief second – just long enough for Adele to ponder what might lie between them.

Then he dropped his head and let himself be helped into the house.

A bustle ensued as he was put to bed on the sofa in the sitting room, with much fuss made over blankets and pillows and stirring up the fire. Adele, slipping comfortably into her professional role, gave clear directions as to what should be done.

"He has an infected wound," she told his mother. "From the looks of it, it's at least a few weeks old, and was not cleaned properly at the time of being inflicted. It will need to be opened up and cleaned out, and then sewn up again. I can do it, but I don't have the proper tools."

Mrs. Wilder – somewhere along the way, Adele had found out that her name was Maria – wrung her hands.

"What shall we do, Nurse Cowen?"

"There's a doctor here in town, isn't there?" The older woman nodded. "I would fetch him to take a look, just to be on the safe side. If my suspicions are correct, then he can provide me with the things I need and I can sew up the wound once it's clean."

She put her hands on her hips, looking down at the prone man. "Then it will just be a case of wait and see – you'll have to keep an eye on it, but he's young and strong. He should recover just fine."

Maria Wilder looked over to the younger woman.

"Annie, will you run and tell James that his brother – that his brother is here. And perhaps he can ride into town and fetch Doctor Miller."

Annie, whose eyes had been fixed on Preston's sleeping face, started suddenly at the sound of her name. She nodded quickly and hurried out.

Maria Wilder gave a deep sigh and reached for Adele's hand.

"Now," she said, leading the way out of the sitting room and toward the kitchen, "I think we're in need of a cup of coffee and a chat. Tell me all about it, my dear."

It had been many years since Adele had last felt so comforted and reassured by the presence of someone older and wiser, and Maria Wilder listened carefully to every bit of her story, with only a brief exclamation now and then. By the time Adele had detailed the train robbery, her abduction by the robbers, and how she had stumbled upon Preston, their coffee had been refilled twice and Mrs. Wilder looked positively exhausted simply by listening to the tale.

"My dear, you must be haggard. You need sleep just as much as my son does. I'll put you up in my bed for now – my other son and his wife live here with me, and we have no spare rooms. There's the cottage outside, of course, but that needs a hearty cleaning and some spider hunting before I'd let a stray dog sleep there. James'll see to it when he gets back. Come along, now, and rest. When you wake up, I'll have some supper for you."

It was on the tip of Adele's tongue to protest that she was not tired, that there was too much to be done – but it would have been a lie. The more she thought about everything that had happened over the last two days, the more tired she became. Wordlessly, then, she followed the kindly older woman down the hallway. She could not help but cast a quick glance into the sitting room as they passed, but Preston was fast asleep on the sofa, his head turned toward the fire.

She was certain that her mind was racing too much for her to be able to sleep, but her body gave out as soon as her head met the pillow. She dreamed of many things, most of them anxious and worrying, fraught with danger – the cold eyes of the bandit above his bandanna, waiting for her to sew up the slice across his temple. The dark settling in overhead as she stood alone in the wilderness. The final look at her empty little flat as she set out for parts unknown.

And through it all, try though she might to avoid it, to change it to mean something else, there was the handsome visage of Preston Wilder, no less handsome in what appeared to be death.

CHAPTER 8

The doctor came and went while Adele was sleeping. So, apparently, did other people; when she finally awoke, it was late at night. There was a cot in the corner, upon which lay the sleeping form of Maria Wilder. Adele sat up straight, heart thumping, and waited for her vision to adjust enough to make out the true nature of the dark shapes around her.

After a moment, her head cleared a little, and she got out of bed noiselessly and padded barefoot to the door.

She found the sitting room with the door ajar, the fire blazing within. The light illuminated the face of Preston Wilder, still sleeping hard but with a peace to him that she had not yet seen. It set the worries of her dream to rest – he was going to recover; she was almost sure of it.

"The doctor said you did a wonderful job, all things considered," said the quiet voice of Annie behind her. Adele clutched a hand to her throat and turned.

"Goodness, you startled me."

Annie smiled.

"I'm sorry – I didn't mean to, but it's hard to announce your presence when the whole house is asleep. Well, apart from the two of us, that is."

"What time is it?"

"Just gone eleven."

Adele put a hand to her forehead. "Goodness."

Annie tilted her head to one side, eyeing Adele curiously. After a moment, she offered, "Would you like something to eat? Maria left a plate in the warmer for you."

It hadn't occurred to her until then, but at the suggestion Adele's stomach rumbled. It had now been nearly two days since she had last eaten.

"It's probably not the best choice to eat so late at night – but yes," she said gratefully. "I'd be obliged."

Annie led the way to the kitchen, sat Adele down at the table, and brought out the plate. It was a shallow bowl of potato soup and a roll of brown bread, obviously baked only that day. In Adele's starving state, it tasted like the most delicious thing she'd ever eaten. Annie sat across from her, sipping a mug of tea.

"Maria told me about your story," she said. "It's a wonder you made it through alive and unharmed."

Adele nodded. "I know – I can scarcely believe it myself."

"I suppose if you hadn't been able to nurse the bandit, things might have been different."

"Perhaps," Adele acknowledged. "Then again, if I hadn't been a nurse, they wouldn't have taken me with them anyhow."

"And then you never would have found Preston," Annie pointed out.

The thought made Adele's heart stop for a moment. Yes, she wouldn't have found him – likely no one would have. He would still be out there, alone in the wilderness, sick and getting sicker by the moment…

Or, even worse, he would have died of the infection, unable to get help.

She shuddered at the thought, and Annie reached out to take her hand.

"We're grateful you made it through," she said. "Though you're a stranger to us, on behalf of my husband James and his mother, I'd like to welcome you to stay with us as long as you like. I hear your husband-to-be is in Texas – we can get you there, when you're ready. But you need time to recover. And…I have a feeling you'd like to see Preston recover, too, before you go."

Adele nodded.

"You're right," she said. "Though I don't know him – though I don't know any of you – I feel rather…invested." She smiled a little. "Perhaps that's just my nature. As a nurse, I like to see things through to the end."

Annie nodded, and there was a curious light in her eyes that made Adele wonder, once more, at the connection between Preston and his sister-in-law. For that matter, what was the bad blood that existed that had kept him from coming home when he was ill? There was a story here, she was certain of it.

"Well," she said, "I hope you're able to get back to sleep. And if you have bad dreams, as I reckon you might – please remember, Adele Cowen, that as far as the Wilders are concerned…you're an angel, and God himself sent you to Preston's side."

She nodded and went out into the hallway, leaving Adele to sit by herself in the warm kitchen, looking after her.

Sleep came easier than she might have thought, even after her long nap through the day and her late night supper. When she awoke again, it was early morning, and Maria was stirring on her cot. The older woman sat up and gave Adele a bright smile.

"Ah, you're awake. I hope you're refreshed, my dear. Do you suppose Preston is awake, too?"

Adele's heart jumped, and she pushed aside the covers.

"I think we should go and find out," she said, suiting action to the word.

Indeed, Preston was awake, though he was clearly still sleepy. When his mother entered the room, he gave her a smile; and to Adele's delight, he then turned the smile on her, as well.

"I don't know that we've been properly introduced," he said. "But I'm glad to know you're not a hallucination after all."

Adele couldn't help but laugh.

"Well, I'm glad that you're glad, Mr. Wilder. Not every girl can say she was mistaken for a hallucination, but it's an exclusive privilege I'm not quite sure about."

Preston reached out a hand, and she took it. Rather than shaking it, as she'd expected, however, he held it carefully, as though she might break.

"I owe you my life," he said. "Couldn't be a greater debt than that, and I know it. Anything you need, Miss Cowen, you have it."

She squeezed his hand, smiling down at him.

"Your thanks is more than enough," she said. "Perhaps you've heard my story already."

"Some of it," he acknowledged.

"Then you know that both of us were fortunate to find each other. I owe you my thanks as well."

He grinned. "Well, I wouldn't say that we're even, but maybe it's getting there. Tell you one thing, though…maybe we should go straight to first names, since we've already spent so much time in company. Call me Preston.'"

"Thank you, I will. And you must call me Adele."

Their eyes met once more and the two of them stayed as they were, hands still joined, smiling a bit foolishly at each other. Adele's heart was positively singing, though she tried desperately to calm it down.

Then suddenly his eyes shifted over her shoulder, toward the door. She turned and saw a man enter. He was a few years older and a bit broader than Preston, but the familial resemblance was clear. This must be James Wilder, Preston's brother.

Behind him, Annie stepped into the room. She glanced briefly at Preston, but it was to Adele that she gave her smile.

"Miss Adele," James said, his voice deep and smoother than Preston's. "I'm mighty pleased to meet you. Annie here has told me she was able to ask you last night about staying with us for a while. However long you like – and when you're ready, we'll get you on to Texas to marry your mayor."

Adele couldn't help but hear the sudden hitch in Preston's breath, couldn't help but feel the brief, unconscious tightening of his grasp. And she couldn't bring herself to turn her head and look at him, either. Evidently, he had not heard all the details of her story.

But then, she hadn't heard all of his, either.

She nodded, keeping her focus on James.

"Yes, Mr. Wilder. Thank you – I'm very pleased to accept your hospitality. I believe that your brother will recover just fine, but it may take a few days. I feel I can be of some help here – and I'd like to see him well and on his feet again before I go."

James gave her a grateful smile. It was nowhere near as attractive as the smile of his younger brother, she noted – but perhaps that was for the best.

"Glad to hear it," he said.

When she turned to Preston, his eyes were fixed on hers once more – but there was something different about his expression now, something almost blank, unreadable, unfathomable. Now he knew the truth about her – and something in him had shut down.

It gave her a sense of loss that she couldn't quite define.

She hoped desperately she had made the right decision in choosing to stay.

CHAPTER 9

Two days passed before Preston Wilder was strong enough to stand and walk on his own. His fever finally abated, and under the steady ministrations of Adele and the watchful eye of his mother, color came back into his cheeks, his appetite returned, and with it his strength.

On the third day after their arrival in the ranch house outside of Fielder's Union, Adele stood near him as he eyed himself critically in the mirror, shaking his head ruefully.

"Three days of beard, and I look like a wild mountain man," he said. "Who's going to take me seriously as a professional if I look this scruffy?"

Adele couldn't help but smile. It was true that he looked a little scruffy – but she could almost believe that the scruffiness was part of the appeal.

"Is it so important to be taken seriously as a professional, in the bounty hunting area of employment?"

"Well," said Preston, reaching for the straight-edge razor and inspecting it for sharpness, "don't you find that it's important to be taken seriously as a nurse?"

"Yes, of course. Although I must admit not everyone does – but that's more due to me being a woman than anything else."

"Women should always be taken seriously," said Preston, meeting her gaze directly. "They're a force to be reckoned with."

There was a heaviness between them, something big and unspoken but meaningful. Adele bit her lip.

"Perhaps if I shaved more often," she blurted out before she could help herself, and was treated with a split-second look of disbelief from Preston before he burst into laughter. She laughed, too, and it felt wonderful—wonderful to share a silly joke with someone that she…

She stopped the thought there, before she could finish it. She couldn't afford to finish it, couldn't afford to admit to herself how she felt. Mayor Franklin Bicknell was waiting for her in Branton, Texas, and she had no right to allow her feelings to be so deeply involved with any other man.

There was no escaping the fact that she and Preston seemed to have a bond, however, and it only strengthened as the days went by. Before she knew it, she had been in Fielder's Union, Arkansas, for a solid week. Days fell into a steady, pleasant pattern. Mornings she went into the kitchen and joined Maria and Annie at cooking and baking for the day. Afternoons, more often than not, she went for a walk with Preston at her side, ostensibly for her protection and his support, but in reality, for the delight that both of them derived from each other's company. She couldn't help but be aware of the continued tension between Preston and his brother, and between Preston and Annie; Preston rarely spoke to either of them, and Adele was uncomfortably certain that, had she the opportunity to judge Preston purely by his relationships with his family, she would believe him to be a cold, distant, and downright rude individual.

But to her he was kind, thoughtful, amusing, and personal. Every once in a while, especially when she mentioned Texas, he would grow quiet once more and avoid her gaze. But the episodes seemed to pass quickly, and he would be back to himself.

He told her stories of becoming a bounty hunter, what it meant, why he had chosen the profession. After several of these in a row, she shook her head.

"It's clear to me," she said, "that your profession is aging you far more quickly than it ought."

"No – you really think so?" He seemed intrigued by her opinion rather than put off, so she expanded.

"Yes. Just look at this wound you have now – am I right in thinking that it isn't the only wound you've ever sustained?"

"I've sustained many wounds over the years," he agreed gravely. "Some gunshot, some knife, some physical, some emotional. Some, I must admit, self-inflicted."

She raised her eyebrows at him but decided to let that comment pass in order to focus on her main theme.

"And you're only twenty-eight years old. Why, I've been a nurse for four years, and I've scarcely seen more violently inflicted wounds in total than you've already had in your career. Besides, aren't you exhausted from chasing outlaws around?"

"I am, at that," he admitted. "I never figured I was cut out for it, exactly – but it was what I chose to do, so I'll keep doing it. For now."

"For now," she echoed, watching him steadily. "Would you like my professional opinion?"

"Please."

"I think it's time you found a new profession. Perhaps one more peaceful." He smiled at her gentle joke. "Or perhaps you could come to work here, with your brother," she suggested. "After all, the ranch is due to be half yours, isn't it?"

But this advice did not elicit the same gentle reaction as her previous words; instead, his face grew rather grim and stony, and he turned away from her.

"Tell me about the gang that robbed the train," he said abruptly, changing the subject. "What did they look like?"

She didn't understand his reluctance to discuss the idea of working on the ranch, but it was clear he would not change his mind. Once more, she ran through the story of the train robbery, answering his specific questions. This time, she mentioned the birthmark on the temple of one of the outlaws, and Preston nodded as though she had confirmed a long-held suspicion.

"That's what I figured," he said. "Your train was held up by the Silver Gang. The one called Chente, that's Vincent Silver, the younger of the two. His brother Mike is the leader. I'd heard they were in the vicinity of Fielder's Union – that's why I was here to begin with." He looked glum. "Maybe I would have caught them if I hadn't been so sick."

"Perhaps," she said, though she had her doubts. "Are you certain that Mike is the leader, Preston?"

"Pretty sure. Why do you ask?"

She explained the odd conversation that the Silver brothers had held just before they left her. "They wouldn't have talked about a 'boss' unless there was someone else telling them what to do, would they?"

"Maybe not," he agreed, rubbing his chin. "Never heard any rumors about anyone else being involved, but there's no reason why not, I guess. Someone orchestrating things, keeping an eye out from the outside – maybe giving them a safe haven to hide out in, in between jobs. It makes sense, now that I think about it. They sure seem to disappear now and then. They must have a pretty good hideout."

"Have you come close to catching them before?"

"I guess you could say that – I've come close, at any rate." He skated a hand over his injured ribs. "Mike Silver's the one who shot me last month."

Adele gaped at him.

"You can't be serious."

"I'm always serious about being shot."

"But – he shot you and you went out again after him anyway?"

Preston shrugged.

"I'm a bounty hunter – that's my job. Besides, a little personal vengeance is an extra reward, isn't it?"

She shook her head. The foolhardiness of chasing after someone who had already shot him, especially when he hadn't even fully recovered from the wound, was startling to her. But it spoke volumes about who Preston was as a person

– stubborn, determined, single-minded, and with a strong sense of justice. Nothing, she knew, was about to stand in his way.

And when he was finally recovered, he would go out after the Silver Gang again.

Impulsively, she reached out and put a hand on his arm.

"Preston, will you promise me that you'll be careful?" She bit her lip. "I may not always be around to help tend to you. I hate to think of… of something happening to you, and I'm not there to save you."

He looked down at her hand on his arm. For the space of a few long, slow breaths, he did not speak.

"Sure," he said, still not looking at her. "I promise – after all, you're right. You won't be around. You'll be in Texas."

The conversation didn't last much longer than that.

The next morning, she slept in later than usual, feeling strangely exhausted after the emotional toll of the last several days. She awoke wondering about Franklin Bicknell – and fighting a guilty conscience. Surely, he must be worried about her. He must have wondered why she hadn't arrived as she should have. She should be on her way to Texas as soon as she could.

She would leave the very next day, she vowed.

Annie was nowhere to be seen when she went down to the kitchen; Maria was there alone, rolling out pie crust. She looked up with a cheerful smile.

"There you are, my dear. You missed breakfast. The boys are out in the fields already, and Annie's gone into town. Would you like something to eat?"

"No, thank you, Maria – I'll just get myself a cup of coffee." She sat at the table, covering a huge yawn with her hand. "Goodness, but I'm so tired today."

"I don't blame you one bit," Maria told her, continuing to work. "You're burning the candle at both ends – helping me at all hours, and then spending all your time with my poor invalid son, getting him back on his feet. Why, you're doing far more than anyone would ever ask or expect of you, my dear."

"Oh, I don't mind any of that. As I've told Preston, it was my good fortune to meet him just as much as it was his to meet me – I can't imagine where I'd be now if I hadn't run into him out there." She took a sip of her coffee. "And I'm glad to know you – all of you. You've all been so kind to me – so kind, I hate to say it, but… I really must be on my way to Texas. Mr. Bicknell will be wondering where I am."

Maria's busy hands stilled for a moment, and she looked up at Adele with a faint sadness in her eyes.

"Are you sure, dear?"

"Yes, I'm sure." It was difficult to say the words; she wanted to retract them as soon as they were out of her mouth. But they were the truth, and she could not in good conscience deny that it was high time to leave. If nothing else, it was a sense of self-preservation – every single day, her feelings for Preston only grew stronger. How much longer before she couldn't muster the self-discipline to leave at all?

"Well, I'm very sorry to hear that." Maria shook her head, returning to her work. "You've been a very pleasant addition to have here – and useful, too. You're good for Preston, too, I must say."

Adele's heart leapt a little. "Good for Preston? What do you mean?"

"I mean he never would have stayed here so long if you weren't at his side," Maria said frankly. "That boy has been gone for six years – six years, without a word except at Christmas, and that just to tell me that he was alive." She shook her head again, tutting to herself. "You'd think that I wasn't the one who raised him, that we had no connection at all, from as little as we see each other."

Adele's face fell.

"That's terrible," she said. "I'm so sorry, Maria – but I know he loves you. I can tell."

"Oh, that's never in question. It isn't me he has a problem with – though it affects me, in the end. It's his brother James, and Annie. I reckon he hasn't told you any of this himself, but under the circumstances I feel you've a right to know as much as anyone else who stays under our roof. Annie was engaged to Preston before she married James – engaged for two weeks. They'd courted for a few months before that. But a little while before the wedding, she told Preston that she was in love with his brother – and of course James was smitten, himself."

Another head shake, the matronly sort that could not quite condone anyone involved but which indicated bemused affection all the same. "I reckon they tried to do things right. I know James fought against his love for Annie – he never wanted to take anything away from his brother, and if Annie had been in love with Preston, James would have gone to his grave keeping his feelings a secret. But the fact is she wasn't, not really – and love has a way of rising to the surface, no matter how hard you try to tamp it down."

She pushed down on the rolling pin, and the dough curled up along the edge, clinging closely in the wake of the pin. Maria sprinkled another dash of flour on the surface and started again.

Adele had a horrible feeling that Maria was right. And if she was, and Adele's feelings for Preston were more than she was ready to admit – was she doomed to a lifetime of pretending to be invested in a marriage to one man while she secretly yearned after another? The thought of her empty life stretching out in front of her, loveless and bitter, made her feel utterly alone.

But it didn't matter, she reminded herself. It wasn't a question of love – it was a question of her moral obligation. She had already thrown one chance at love away by agreeing to live with Gerald – was it only a few short months ago? So much had happened since then. It was startling to realize. She could not in good conscience decide to reject the agreement she'd come to with Franklin Bicknell, not now that she had been given another chance.

Even if it caused her a lifetime of sorrow and regret, she could not back down.

It seemed almost as though Maria was aware of the tender of her thoughts, for she gave Adele a long, thoughtful look.

"It's too bad you're engaged to be married," she said. "I hope you don't mind me saying so, but – I doubt Preston could find someone better suited to him. And I wouldn't mind having a daughter-in-law like you."

Unexpectedly, the simple words brought tears to Adele's eyes.

"That's very sweet of you," she managed. "But I'm afraid I'm obligated…"

"You're certain nothing will change your mind?" Maria's eyes met hers keenly. Though it felt like a heavy weight on her shoulders, Adele shook her head.

"No, nothing," she said. "It isn't that – it isn't that I mind the idea, not at all. I like your son very much. But – I've already given my word. And Mr. Bicknell has done nothing to betray my trust in him; how can I do otherwise?"

It was a helpless situation, and Adele despised feeling helpless. If someone else were hurting, she would rush in, doing everything she could to help. But it was just an emotional wound, and she herself was the victim. There was nothing to be done about it. Nothing at all.

Overcome and unable to speak, she turned and went down the hallway. She found her way out onto the veranda at the back of the house and went around the corner to sit on the porch bench. It was quiet and secluded there, and she sat for a long time in silence, her mind racing through the same subjects over and over, no sooner touching on one than darting on to the next. She had an obligation to keep. She could not stay here. She could not marry Preston – nor could she deny her love for him.

As the sun rose high overhead on the bright spring day, she felt the hair at the nape of her neck prickle. Turning her head, she saw Preston himself, standing just at the edge of the porch, almost hidden around the corner. He must have crept up on her silently; the kind of skill that would come in handy for a bounty hunter, she thought bitterly. Now she understood why he was so adamant about not staying here on the ranch. Now she understood his strained relationship with his brother. Betrayal was a strong force – but should not love be stronger? It had been six years, and though she sympathized with his hurt, she couldn't help but judge him for not moving on.

Was he still in love with Annie? Was that the problem, the issue that held him back?

But as her eyes met his, dark and full of meaning, she couldn't believe it.

She swallowed hard and stood up.

"I'm going to Texas," she said. "I've got to go. Will you help me?"

Preston stepped forward. "You're leaving?"

"You knew that I would."

Another step.

"I thought you might change your mind."

It was on the tip of her tongue to tell him that his mother had evidently believed the same thing. Perhaps his brother, too, perhaps his sister-in-law. Perhaps the entire family was aware of the fact that Adele Cowen was hopelessly in love with Preston Wilder, and everyone assumed she would set aside her previous obligation and troth herself to him instead. Well, everyone was mistaken.

"You thought wrong," she said.

"Do you want to go to Texas?"

She fought back a sob, bringing her arms out to her sides in a gesture of futility. "What choice do I have?"

Preston reached out and took her hands in his.

"Stay here," he said. "With me. I'll retire from hunting – I'll make amends with my brother – we can live in the cottage and work on the ranch. You can go to work for Doc Miller, he'd be delighted to have a nurse like you. We'd be happy."

She shook her head, biting her lip. "I can't."

"You and me, Adele – we met in the middle of nowhere, in the middle of the night. I was sick, you were abducted and abandoned alone – we saved each other, didn't we? Don't you think that means something?"

She looked up into his eyes, and the words she wanted to speak died on her lips. He bent down to kiss her, letting go of her hands and slipping his arms around her waist. She clung to him for a moment before she put the heels of her hands on his shoulders and pushed him back.

"I must leave," she said, shaken but firm. "Tomorrow. Tell me you'll help me to get there, Preston – tell me you'll see me there safely. Promise me."

Preston Wilder was quiet for a moment, and then his eyes went blank and unreadable as they had done before. He dropped his hands from her waist.

"I promise," he said. He turned and walked away, leaving her to stand on the porch alone in the bright sunshine of the beautiful spring day.

CHAPTER 10

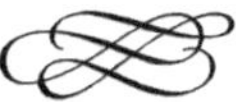

The sun was up early the next morning, and everyone in the Wilder ranch house got up along with it. There was much bustle in the kitchen as food was made and wrapped up to be taken along, and Annie helped Adele to pack the few clothes and belongings she'd accumulated over the past week, all donated by kindly neighbors who had been made aware of the situation. James pulled Preston aside as he saddled the horse.

"I meant what I told you," the older man said, a bit stiffly even now. "If you would consider coming back here to live, there's always a place for you."

"I heard you the first time you told me about it, yesterday morning."

"And you know Ma would be delighted to have you around. She misses you. Worries about you."

"That's Ma's nature. If I was here, she'd find something else to worry about."

James rubbed the back of his neck.

"I miss you, too," he admitted. "It's been a long time, Preston. I'll keep saying I'm sorry for hurting you for as long as it takes – till the day I die, if need be. It won't change anything, though. Only you can change how you feel."

Preston slipped the reins over the horse's head, pondering his brother's words. He had been so reluctant to come back here to the ranch. He could remember a time, not long ago, that he had sworn he wouldn't be caught dead here. Well, he very nearly had been. If Adele hadn't been the one to find him, hadn't agreed to stay and take care of him, nurse him back to health…

Somehow, in the week since he'd arrived back at the Wilder ranch, the dread he had felt had disappeared. Along with it had gone most of his animosity toward his brother and his wife. Granted, nothing could entirely lessen the sting of the betrayal. But, after all, it had been six years.

And James was right. Preston was the only one who could change how he felt.

Well – with Adele's help, anyhow.

He looked at his brother, feeling a warmth and compassion that had been gone for far too long.

"I'll think about it," he said. "Can't say fairer than that. I know it'd be good for Ma to have us both here as she gets older."

James nodded, and his smile turned a little sheepish.

"Besides, you were always her favorite," he said.

"Oh, go on with you. You reminded her of herself, that's why she liked you so well."

"And you remind her of Pa – that's why she likes you best."

The two brothers grinned at each other for a moment.

"When were you going to tell me Annie's expecting?"

"Oh, gosh," said James, blushing bright red. He clapped a hand to his forehead. "Who told you? It was Mrs. Brown, wasn't it?"

"No one told me, I figured it out for myself. I may be a bachelor, James, but I'm not a complete fool. It's about time you started a family."

"Well," muttered James, rubbing at his neck again. "I had meant to tell you – just never seemed the right time. And I wasn't sure how…how you'd take it, you know."

"I know," Preston said, turning away from him again. "I know."

James sighed and clapped his younger brother on the shoulder.

"Come back after you get her to Texas, will you?"

Preston nodded.

"I can't promise I'll stay, but… I think I can promise that much."

Adele came out onto the veranda, a small bag in her hand and another slung over her shoulder. She gave Preston a somewhat watery smile. His heart leapt at the sight of her – her beauty, her bravery. Why was she leaving?

Because she was engaged to another man, he told himself sternly. And because she was a better woman than he had any right to expect for himself.

"You ready?" he asked quietly.

Her eyes were filled with tears.

"No," she said. "So we'd better hurry."

In the interests of getting to Branton as quickly as possible, they had agreed to take James' fastest horse rather than hitching up and going in the wagon. Preston mounted the saddle and then reached down, bringing Adele up behind him. She put her arms around him, and he felt her press her cheek against his back. It was a temporary admission of her feelings that touched his heart; he knew she would never admit to her affection for him, not while she was engaged to another man. But she was glad to have him while she could, and the pressure of her body against his was as exquisitely torturous as their kiss had been, the day before.

The day passed swiftly, filled with nothing but the sound of the horse's hooves and the air streaming by. They made good time, thundering through the few towns that stood between Fielder's Union and Branton, stopping only a few times. It was nearing three o'clock when they arrived at the outskirts of Branton, Texas. The town wasn't far over the border, for which Preston was grateful; he couldn't imagine the difficulty of taking Adele far away, of being forced to share a room at the inn overnight, perhaps...

A quick inquiry at the mercantile directed them to the mayoral residence. It was a large house at the northeast end of town, painted a rather startling pink. It stood on an extensive lot, with a small stable at the back. Everything about it spoke of affluence, of the sort that was rather surprising for a small-town mayor. Perhaps, Preston thought disinterestedly, he had an inheritance. It didn't matter, he figured, as long as the man took good care of Adele.

As they drew closer and closer, Preston brought the horse to a canter, and then to a walk – and then to a stop. They weren't more than fifty feet from the gate leading up to the veranda, but he knew that he could go no further without once more begging Adele to change her mind.

"I'd better leave you here," he said. "Don't want your husband-to-be to get suspicious or anything."

Adele sucked in a breath as though the knowledge they were separating for good had suddenly hit her.

"Yes – yes, of course. You're right."

He slid down from the horse and handed her down. For the briefest of moments, his hands stayed on her waist, their eyes locked. She trembled slightly beneath his hands. Then he turned his head and looked away.

"I wish you happiness," he said.

Adele pressed her lips together.

"And you," she said. "Please – take care of yourself, Preston."

He nodded but could say nothing else. He kept his eyes turned away until he was certain she was at the gate, her back to him; then, unable to help himself, he looked up at last. She opened the gate and passed through, head up, shoulders back, brave as the day she had first come into his life. Preston knew in his heart he would never again meet anyone quite like Adele Cowen.

And it broke his heart to know he would never see her again.

He couldn't bring himself to leave, even after he watched her knock on the door and be admitted into the large house. It was a nice place, he had to admit – under the guise of investigating it to ensure she would be properly taken care of, he mounted the horse and rode around the grounds for a while, taking it all in. Everything was well-kept. This mayor fellow must have a staff of at least ten to keep everything in such good repair, and so clean.

Preston hadn't figured on mayor-ing being such a lucrative profession; but then again, maybe it didn't matter when it came to the important things. After all, as rich as the man must be, he still had been unable to find a wife amongst his own townspeople. He'd had to write far away to New York, placing an advertisement in the paper for someone who didn't know him…

It gave Preston a funny feeling in the pit of his stomach. He dismissed it as sheer jealousy – after all, he knew he was jealous. There was no point in denying it. Still, the idea that no one wanted to marry this rich mayor couldn't help but make a man wonder about his character…

And then he saw his horse.

"Major."

There was no doubt about it. Major wore a strange saddle, with a shotgun clearly strapped along his side, as though he'd been ridden by a hunter. Even so, Preston would have known that fine figure anywhere – but the truth was undeniable when the horse immediately turned his head to seek out his erstwhile master, trotting to the gate at the edge of the corral and leaning his long, sleek neck over to try and reach him. Preston slid out of the saddle and ran to his horse, flinging his arms about his neck. The animal tossed his head briefly but submitted to the embrace. Preston stepped back, half unable to believe his eyes.

"How on earth did you end up…here…"

The truth hit him with all the force of a bullet.

CHAPTER 11

Adele waited in the sitting room. It was nicely appointed, easily the most richly-decorated room she'd ever been in. The mantlepiece was made of well-polished mahogany, with a fire blazing merrily in its stone depths; two expensive-looking vases rested on the shelf. Adele stood with her back to it, standing at the window, trying to keep her breathing under control – and push away the intense feeling of sadness that threatened to swamp her with every breath. She had said goodbye to Preston Wilder, never to see him again. She was keeping her word, and that must be her consolation.

Now, there was nothing to do but wait until her husband-to-be arrived, and she was finally able to meet the man she had agreed to marry.

The housekeeper seemed nice enough, though she bore a frown that was apparently permanent, etching a line between her eyebrows. The maid who had hurried by in the hall seemed polite, too, though her expression was much the same. There was an aura in this house, Adele couldn't help but think, that seemed to hint at repressed secrets. But surely, she was just imagining things. Surely it was just a case of searching for a way out of doing her duty and keeping her word…

Repressed secrets, worried house staff, unknown complexities beneath the surface, mysterious mayors – all of that was the stuff of novels, wasn't it? Just like – she caught herself and chuckled, despite her sadness. Just like arranged marriages, Mail Order Brides, train robberies, and nursing handsome men back to health.

For the first time, she wondered whether she had somehow stumbled into the middle of a romance novel herself.

Then the door opened, distracting her from her thoughts. She whirled around to see a tall, somewhat portly man enter the room. He gave her a smile – overall, he seemed harmless enough, though he certainly was nowhere near as attractive as… as, well, some men she could think of…

"Miss Cowen. I'm so very happy you've made it at last. I was beginning to wonder."

"Mr. Bicknell," she greeted him, and he took her hand in a rather limp grasp.

"Mayor Bicknell, please – at least, until we get to know each other. Then, I'm sure, we'll both feel comfortable with first names." He had a chuckle so rich it seemed to be swimming in gravy. He held out a hand to her, inviting her to sit down, and took a seat opposite her. He still had possession of her hand. "Now, please, do tell me what on earth happened on the way here. I had sent my kitchen boy to collect you at the station, and you were nowhere to be found."

"Well, Mr. – I mean, Mayor Bicknell, the truth may rather shock you. My train was stopped by bandits, and then I was abducted and forced to nurse one of the outlaws."

Mayor Bicknell eyed her, then sat back, rubbing his chin.

"Outlaw attacks, forced abductions," he said. "That sounds rather outlandish, Miss Cowen. We don't usually have such occurrences here – I would venture to say that Branton is the safest town in the United States."

"I'm sure, Mayor Bicknell," she said, feeling rather stung by his obvious skepticism. "But this didn't happen here. It happened a day's journey away – just outside of a town called Fielder's Union, Arkansas."

The man's eyebrows raised as smoothly as though they had been oiled. He was losing his hair, she noted – both on his head, and in his brows. In the warm spring weather, his skin had the consistency and sheen of a hardboiled egg.

"Fielder's Union?"

"Have you heard of it?"

"Not at all," he said immediately. "I very rarely take any interest in any town that isn't Branton – Branton is the best, the only place to be. You've made a very wise decision in choosing to come here. No more train robberies for you, my dear, that I can promise you."

She tilted her head, taken aback by his odd words and unsure of what to make of them.

"Surely no one can guarantee such things won't happen," she said.

"Not with me at your side," he said, thumping his chest proudly and coughing a little. "My name and reputation will protect you – and anywhere you go, you will have a bodyguard." He turned to the door, waving at someone she could not see. "In fact, perhaps you'd like to meet some of my staff right now – you'll see them quite often, my dear, so you should become acquainted with their faces…"

Two tall, rangy men came in. One was clearly a little older than the other, with dark hair slicing across his forehead. The other also had dark hair, but his features were marred somewhat by the long cut down his face. The upper portion of it had been expertly tended to and sewn – she would have recognized her own handiwork anywhere. Beneath it, a circular birthmark slipped into a narrow curve at the end, completing the shape of a kidney and reaching nearly down to his jaw. The two looked enough alike to be brothers; they shared the same dark hair, the same cold eyes.

Adele's heart was in her throat, and she sat paralyzed as the two turned to face her. There was an instant flare of mingled shock and recognition, and the younger of the two – Vincent Silver – drew his pistol and pointed it at her.

"You."

"Wait." Mike Silver reached out, pushing his brother's hand down. He frowned at Adele in consternation. "What in God's name are you doing here? Wasn't it enough that we let you go free? Why would you be so stupid as to try and hunt us down?"

Mayor Bicknell was on his feet, frowning mightily. "What's going on here?"

Adele got to her own feet, clutching her hands in front of her to keep them from trembling.

"Mayor Bicknell," she said, "I'm sorry to have to tell you this – but your staff are not who you think they are. These two men are the ones who robbed the train I was on. They are Mike and Vincent Silver, and they lead the Silver Gang."

Mayor Bicknell heaved a sigh.

"Ah. I see," he said quietly. He turned to Mike Silver. "Gentlemen, I expect a full explanation of this most unusual occurrence, in due time. Meanwhile, I suppose

Miss Cowen is too dangerous to be allowed to remain alive."

Adele cried out. Vincent raised his hand again, but his brother grabbed him once more.

"Come on, boss," he said. "Didn't she just get here? Isn't she the lady you wrote for? Why not give her a try, see whether she'll play ball with us. You won't turn us in, will you, nursey?" he asked Adele. "Maybe we can get to some agreement."

Mayor Bicknell shook his head. "Regrettably, Mike, your softer instincts are getting in the way of action once more. Honestly, how many times must I tell you?"

"One of these days, folks are going to notice that people go missing around here," Mike Silver argued. "This isn't the first time you've tried to find a wife – you keep making girls disappear like this, and people'll get suspicious. Then it's goodbye to the good life. That ain't what you want, is it?"

Once more, the mayor of Branton, Texas, heaved a sigh.

"Perhaps you're right, Mike – perhaps we will have to alter course next time. Or perhaps – just perhaps – next time you'll refrain from showing yourself to my bride-to-be, hmm?" His tone was acid. "This is your fault, Mike, not mine. Her death can be on your conscience, if you like."

He nodded to Vincent, who wrested his arm away from his older brother and raised the gun again.

"For now, she's too much trouble to keep alive. Too bad, too bad – she is terribly pretty."

Adele's eyes met Vincent's, briefly, wildly. She'd seen those eyes before, watching her as she stitched up his wound. She had helped him, kept him from dying of blood poisoning – if there was anything human in him, he wouldn't hurt her, not after all she had done…

But his eyes were cold, and his finger only tightened on the trigger.

The sound of the gunshot rocked through her like an earthquake. She squeezed her eyes shut, holding her breath, and everything was silent. Then there was a ringing in her ears, and the world rushed away from her. She opened her eyes and knew that she was not hurt. It was Vincent Silver who lay prone on the ground. The blast had turned him around so that he lay with his face up, his cold eyes staring unblinkingly at the ceiling.

There came an unfamiliar sound, and her eyes darted toward the source of it. Preston Wilder stood in the doorway, holding a rifle. His eyes sought hers, but just briefly; then they returned to the mayor and Mike Silver.

"Now you know, gentlemen," he said slowly, "that I mean business. Put your hands on your heads and get down on your knees." He aimed the gun at them. "Now."

Wordlessly, Mike Silver did as he was told. Mayor Bicknell, however, took a step forward.

"I don't know who you think you are, mister," he said, "but you can't barge into my house like this and shoot my staff without facing the consequences. I'm the mayor of this town, I'll have you know."

Preston gave a half grin.

"Believe me," he said. "I know."

He glanced to the side as the housekeeper hurried into view.

"Get the sheriff," he ordered, and she scurried off obediently.

That moment of distraction had been just enough. Franklin Bicknell lunged forward, grappling for the shotgun, the two men connected by their holds on the barrel, the gun between them. It went off, shattering a vase on the mantlepiece. Adele gave a cry of terror. Still on his knees with his hands on his head, Mike Silver watched with interest.

Preston was the stronger of the two, but the mayor was bigger. By sheer bulk he managed to pressure the younger man over onto his back, knocking him to the ground and pressing the gun against his throat. Adele grabbed at her own throat, feeling the choking sensation that throbbed with every ragged breath that Preston drew. She had to do something, something – anything. But what could she do? She was a nurse – she wanted nothing more than to help people who needed her – she wasn't trained to protect herself or anyone else from evil men.

But she couldn't simply stand by and watch as Preston was killed.

Her breath came faster and faster, her heart pumping so quickly she was half afraid she would have an attack. In a blur, only slightly aware of her actions, she ran to the mantlepiece. One of the vases was in pieces, but the other was intact – for the moment. It was large and heavy, the side of it at least three inches thick.

It would have to do.

Lifting it over her head, she brought it down on the shiny, balding head of Mayor Franklin Bicknell.

The sound made her ill, and the vase broke into several pieces in her hands, falling around him like rain. Bicknell gave a slight moan and went over sideways, falling limp. Adele put her hands to her mouth, eyes wide. At her feet, Preston Wilder pushed aside the gun and sat up slowly, recovering his breath. He looked up at her, and his eyes were filled with love.

She gave him a hand, and helped him up, wrapping her arm around him to support him, much as she had done shortly after they'd first met. For several long moments they stood there, embraced, intertwined, unwilling to let go.

"Shh," he whispered. "Don't cry, Adele."

"I'm not," she said, pulling back a little. "Though it's as much of a surprise to me as it is to you. Do you think I killed him? I'm afraid to check."

"No, no, I can see him breathing. He'll just take a nice little sleep for a while – and hopefully wake up in time for the sheriff to take him off to jail." He looked over her head to the place where Mike Silver had so recently been waiting patiently and heaved a sigh. The window was open, and the outlaw leader was nowhere to be seen. "Guess I won't be collecting that bounty."

She hugged him fiercely.

"I know he has done many bad things – but he did try to stop them from shooting me. That must count for something."

"It counts for a lot," said Preston fervently.

"Will you – will you leave him, then? Let someone else bring him in, if they can."

Preston hesitated, and she knew it must be rather painful to him to be so unprofessional. But after a moment, he nodded.

"I will," he said. "Someone else can collect the bounty – besides, the price is for the leader of the Silver Gang." He gestured to the prone body of the mayor beneath them. "And we've got him right here."

"Oh, Preston – it seems too strange to be true."

"As strange as a nurse stumbling upon a sick man in the middle of nowhere?" Preston asked gently, lifting her chin with his finger until she met his gaze.

"What are we going to do now?" she whispered.

He smiled.

"Well," he said, "I thought, to start with…"

This kiss was expected, anticipated – but no less wonderful for all that. She clung to him tightly and buried her face in the crook of his neck when they parted at last.

"Was it all a coincidence?" she murmured. "You and me, meeting as we did. The Silver Gang, robbing the train I was on. And now, Franklin Bicknell, the man I was supposed to marry, turning out to be the leader of the gang after all. Was it just happenstance, how things turned out?"

"I don't like to call it coincidence," said Preston, thoughtfully. "But I don't know what else to call it – except, maybe, a kind and benevolent Creator, looking out for us foolish humans down here on earth."

He kissed her again, lightly, and put his arm around her once more, turning her to look out the open window. The sun was beginning to set; by nightfall, the mayor would be behind bars. And perhaps, she thought, they would be on their way home – home, back to Wilder Ranch in Fielder's Union. She wouldn't mind riding through the night, if it got them there all the sooner.

"God watching out for us… That's what I'd like to believe, anyway. I don't want to think anything so fragile as coincidence brought you to me."

"What about luck, then?" she suggested. Preston Wilder smiled, holding onto her all the more tightly.

"Luck," he said. "All right. We could call it luck. But truly, I think it was God above."

She smiled at him, and together, they waited for the sunset.

The End

CONTINUE READING...

Thank you for reading *The Nurse Finds Love* Are you wondering **what to read next?** Why not read *Swapping His Bride?* **Here's a peek for you:**

The soft summer sun of an early spring day lit up the landscape around Circle Moss, and the verdant green of the pastures seemed to glow in the light. Far off to the south, longhorn cattle lowed and champed, seeming small and easy to manage in the distance. The ranch was peaceful, waking up from the long winter and welcoming the foretaste of summer heat.

Adrian Moss, his arms folded, and his narrow frame leaned back against the side of the barn, smiled at the sight, but it was more from habit than anything. His hazel green eyes scarcely saw the details of the beauty in front of him. He was contemplating a different sort of beauty – the beauty of the woman he was going to marry.

The fact he had not yet seen her in person meant little. He was sure she would be beautiful, just as he was sure they would love each other dearly as soon as they laid eyes on each other. How could it be any other way?

That, at least, was what the agency would have him believe.

Mrs. Gibbons, of the Gibbons and MacNenny Matrimonial Agency over in Hamilton, had assured him of as much, many times over.

"We are in the business of making matches that are not just a matter of a husband in need of a wife, Mr. Moss," she had told him, chin lifting and nostrils flaring with the glory and honor of her chosen profession. "We are in the business of making matches that result in the union of two souls."

Mrs. Gibbons' flowery expressions notwithstanding, Adrian had to admit to himself the idea was immensely appealing. Here he was, twenty-eight years old and one of a scattered handful of men his age in the area who had not yet found a wife, settled down, and started a family. Unmarried women in and around Fort Riggins, Montana, were at a premium due to their rarity. Even widows below forty were highly prized. Any girl who had a husband who was accident-prone or a bit on the sickly side was kept note of, just in case. It made sense, overall, that the matrimonial agency would open up in Hamilton, the county seat. Word had gotten around, as it tended to do in small communities without many hobbies readily available, and before long, Adrian's foreman, Stu Demont, was nudging Adrian in the ribs and saying, "What do you reckon, Ade? 'Bout time that we settled down?"

Adrian couldn't help but grin at the memory. His foreman was a few years older than Adrian himself, and even more settled a bachelor.

Visit HERE To Read More!

https://ticahousepublishing.com/mail-order-brides.html

MORE MAIL ORDER BRIDE ROMANCES FOR YOU!

We love clean, sweet, adventurous Mail Order Bride Romances and have a lovely library of Susannah Calloway titles just for you!

Box Sets — A Wonderful Bargain for You!

https://ticahousepublishing.com/bargains-mob-box-sets.html

Or enjoy Susannah's single titles. You're sure to find many favorites! (Remember all of them can be downloaded FREE with Kindle Unlimited!)

Sweet Mail Order Bride Romances!

https://ticahousepublishing.com/mail-order-brides.html

ABOUT THE AUTHOR

Susannah has always been intrigued with the Western movement - prairie days, mail-order brides, the gold rush, frontier life! As a writer, she's excited to combine her love of story with her love of all that is Western. Presently, Susannah lives in Wyoming with her hubby and their three amazing children.

www.ticahousepublishing.com
contact@ticahousepublishing.com